Kidnapped!

The huge balloon glided along the ground. A stiff breeze was blowing it straight into Flossie's path.

"Something's wrong!" Bert started running forward.

But the balloon was already in front of Flossie. She stopped in surprise.

Then a man popped up in the gondola. His long arms shot out and grabbed Flossie!

Bert, Nan, and Freddie were too far away. They all watched helplessly as Flossie was pulled into the gondola.

"Help!" she yelled. "Let go of me!"

Books in The New Bobbsey Twins series:

#1   The Secret of Jungle Park
#2   The Case of the Runaway Money
#3   The Clue That Flew Away

Available from MINSTREL Books

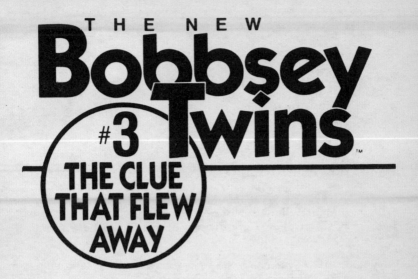

THE NEW
Bobbsey Twins
Twins
#3
THE CLUE THAT FLEW AWAY

LAURA LEE HOPE

ILLUSTRATED BY GEORGE TSUI

A MINSTREL™ BOOK

PUBLISHED BY POCKET BOOKS

This novel is a work of fiction. Names, characters, places and incidents are either the product of the author's imagination or are used fictitiously. Any resemblance to actual events or locales or persons, living or dead, is entirely coincidental.

A MINSTREL PAPERBACK *ORIGINAL*

 A Minstrel Book published by
POCKET BOOKS, a division of Simon & Schuster, Inc.,
1230 Avenue of the Americas, New York, N.Y. 10020

ISBN: 0-671-62653-1

Produced by Mega-Books of New York, Inc.

First Minstrel Books printing December, 1987

10 9 8 7 6 5 4 3 2 1

THE NEW BOBBSEY TWINS, A MINSTREL BOOK and colophon
are trademarks of Simon & Schuster, Inc.

THE BOBBSEY TWINS is a registered trademark
of Simon & Schuster, Inc.

Printed in the U.S.A.

Contents

1. Going to a Party 1

2. To Catch a Thief 12

3. Quiet on the Set! 19

4. A Scary Stunt 28

5. Timber! 36

6. Action! 44

7. A Yellow Clue 53

8. Up, Up, and Away 60

9. A Crash Course in Flying 68

10. Touchdown 78

THE CLUE
THAT FLEW
AWAY

1

Going to a Party

"Amy Armstrong has all the luck," Flossie Bobbsey complained. "She gets a birthday party with movie stars."

"Well, you only turn twelve once." Nan Bobbsey grinned at her younger sister.

"The movie stars didn't come to Lakeport for Amy's birthday. You don't know anything, Flossie," said Freddie, Flossie's twin brother. "They're here for the movie that's being shot in town—*The Great Balloon Race.*"

He peered out the window of the Bobbseys' station wagon, squinting up into the glaring sunset. "Maybe they'll be giving balloon rides at the party. I'd like *that.*"

"Well, we'll find out in a minute," their father said. He pulled up at the end of a long line of cars outside the Armstrong estate.

"Hey, Dad, there's a guard at the gate," Bert Bobbsey said. "He's checking everyone against a guest list. I hope you brought our invitation, Nan," he said, teasing his twin sister.

Amy was Nan's friend from school. She had invited all her classmates—and their families— to her party. But Mrs. Bobbsey was there to work, too. She was a reporter and planned to do a story about the party for the *Lakeport News.*

It was really two parties. One was for the kids—to celebrate Amy's birthday. The other was for the grown-ups, to meet the stars of the movie.

"This is going to be some night," said Mr. Bobbsey.

"But we may end up spending all of it outside," said Bert. "This line isn't moving."

Finally, they made their way to the gate. The guard checked off their names on his list. "Go ahead," he said.

They drove up the long, winding lane leading to the mansion. The Armstrong estate was huge—it had twenty acres of woods and gardens surrounding the house. "Don't you wish we could live in a house like this!" Flossie exclaimed.

"Oh, it's not so great," Nan said. "Sometimes Amy gets pretty lonely. There aren't any other kids nearby, and her dad is away a lot on business. He won't even be here for her birthday party."

Finally, the Bobbseys reached the circular drive in front of the mansion. They got out of their station wagon and left it to be parked by a man in uniform.

Excited kids dashed back and forth on the front lawn. In between, knots of adults stood and chatted.

"I'm so glad you could come," Mrs. Lilian Armstrong said. She shook hands with Mr. and Mrs. Bobbsey, and smiled at the twins. "You're just in time for our guests of honor—real movie stars."

A big limousine pulled up at the marble steps of the mansion. The door opened, and a teenage boy got out. He was handsome, with thick black hair and a bright smile. People began clapping, especially some of the older girls. One of them was Nan.

"That's Tim Archer," Flossie spoke up. "I heard Nan talking about him with her friends on the phone." Her eyes twinkled wickedly. "She's in love with him."

Nan's cheeks burned, and she stopped clapping. "Flossie!" she hissed.

Tim Archer went up the marble stairs, smiling and waving.

Another limousine pulled up, and a man got out. "Is that another star?" Freddie asked.

"No, he's the director of the film—Ross Benton," Mrs. Bobbsey said. "I hope to get a few words from him tonight."

Ross Benton turned to the open limousine door and offered his hand. A little girl got out.

Freddie blinked. "I don't believe it!" he said. "She looks like Flossie!"

"That must be Jessica Jordon," said Mrs. Bobbsey. "She's starring in the film, too."

"But she looks *exactly* like Flossie," Freddie said. "Is this a horror movie?" Then he said, "Oof!" as Flossie poked him with her elbow.

Jessica gave a shy smile and waved at everyone.

Ross Benton faced the crowd and spoke in a loud voice. "As director of *The Great Balloon Race,* I'd like to thank Mrs. Armstrong. We appreciate her help especially in allowing us to use the Armstrong Flyer. It will appear as the grand prize in our movie."

"What's the Armstrong Flyer?" Flossie wanted to know.

"A model hot-air balloon," said Mrs. Bobbsey. "It's made of gold and jewels, and it's very valuable. The movie is about a cross-country balloon race. They're using the Armstrong Flyer as the winner's prize."

"So," Benton went on, "since she lent us her balloon, we brought her one of ours."

Then a voice cried, "Look!"

A chorus of "Ooohs!" and "Ahs!" went up as everyone stared at the sky. Floating overhead was a huge rainbow-colored hot-air balloon. A big, silver-haired man operated the balloon, bringing it down to a perfect landing.

"There *will* be balloon rides!" Freddie said excitedly.

"This is the Rainbow Clipper. It's one of the balloons we're using in *The Great Balloon Race,*" Benton said. "It will float fifty feet above us for the party."

"Float?" Freddie burst out. "No rides? What a dumb idea!" He spoke much louder than he meant to. Lots of people heard and chuckled.

Ross Benton pretended not to notice. He gave orders to the crew, who began to attach ropes to the balloon. At the other end they fastened heavy weights to the ropes. The balloon rose again, with the ropes trailing from it. Higher and higher it went, until the ropes became taut. Then the balloon bobbed a little, like a toy balloon on a string.

Everyone clapped as the beautiful Rainbow Clipper floated in the air.

"And now," Mrs. Armstrong said, raising her voice, "I understand there's a party set up inside." Everybody went in.

Delighted cries came from the kids. "Balloons!" Each child received a party favor—a helium-filled balloon with a small wicker basket hanging beneath. "Just like the one outside," Bert said.

"Now, you have your choice," said Mrs. Armstrong. "Games in the playroom or dancing in the ballroom."

Bert, Freddie, and Flossie ran for the playroom. But Nan hesitated at the ballroom door, where all the grown-ups had gone.

A flashbulb went off. Nan turned to see Mrs. Armstrong posing for a photographer from the *News*. She held the Armstrong Flyer. The model balloon was almost four inches high, made of dark blue china set with hundreds of tiny diamonds and rubies. Gold wires encircled it, and led down to a basket made of spun gold.

"Wow!" Nan whispered. "It must be worth a fortune."

"Nan!" Amy Armstrong called. "I have someone I want you to meet."

Nan walked into the ballroom. She started to

wish Amy a happy birthday, then froze when she saw who was with her. "This is my friend Nan Bobbsey," Amy said. "And, Nan, I think you know Tim Archer."

"W-well, I've seen all his movies," Nan said.

Tim smiled at her. "Nice to meet you."

"Oh, Amy, dear," called Mrs. Armstrong. "We'd like to get a photograph of you holding the Flyer." Amy hurried off. Nan was alone with Tim.

"Nice music," Tim Archer said as the band started playing.

I'll die if he asks me to dance, Nan thought.

"Would you like to dance?"

"Um, okay," Nan said.

Bert arrived at the ballroom to see his sister and Tim in the middle of a slow dance. Nan had a big smile on her face. She looked as if she couldn't believe what was happening to her.

Then her smile vanished. A woman in her twenties with long, chestnut-colored hair had walked up to them. She tapped Nan on the shoulder to cut in on the dance.

"Lara!" Tim said.

"Don't tell me you forgot," Lara said. "You promised me the first dance yesterday on the set."

"Um, well," Tim said. "Okay."

Nan's face was red as she stepped away. Lara quickly moved into the young actor's arms, dancing with him cheek to cheek. Nan couldn't help watching Tim and Lara as they danced. They're exactly the same height—a perfect match, she thought. And Lara is so pretty.

Bert came up to Nan. "Let's get a soda or something," he suggested. As they went to the refreshment table, they bumped into Freddie and Chip Armstrong, Amy's younger brother. Both carried plates piled high with food.

"Why are you loading up like that?" Bert asked.

"We're going to hide out in Chip's room and play computer games," Freddie explained. "Before Flossie makes us dance." He made a disgusted face. "See you later. And don't tell on us."

Bert and Nan both laughed as they watched the two boys sneak off.

"Wait till you see my new computer game," Chip told Freddie on the way upstairs to his room. "It's called Cosmic Destroyer. You blow up planets and everything!"

"Great!" Freddie said. They passed a big, round window at the landing of the stairs. Freddie stopped. "Look!" he said. One of the party-favor balloons floated slowly past the window. "I guess somebody let it get away," he said.

"Too bad," Chip said. "Uh-oh. Flossie's at the bottom of the stairs. Let's get out of here before she sees us." They ran up the steps.

Bert and Nan caught Flossie before she could follow the boys. They took her into the playroom and left her with some younger kids. Then they joined a group of their friends.

After half an hour, Nan felt restless. She stepped outside to look at the Rainbow Clipper floating overhead, and found her father talking with Mrs. Armstrong. She smiled at Nan. "Having a good time?"

"Oh, yes," Nan said. A flash of green against Mrs. Armstrong's dark dress caught Nan's eye. "That's a beautiful necklace you're wearing."

"Why, thank you, dear." Mrs. Armstrong ran a finger along her emerald necklace, straightening it. Then a worried look passed over her face.

"Oh, dear. I hope I locked the door to my room. I left the Flyer up there—with my diamond bracelet and some rings." She hurried away, calling back, "Excuse me, while I check."

Moments later, Nan and Mr. Bobbsey heard a piercing scream. They quickly raced into the house, and met Bert running from the play-room.

Mrs. Armstrong was clinging to the banister at the top of the stairs.

"It's gone!" she sobbed. "Someone has stolen the Armstrong Flyer!"

2

To Catch a Thief

Mrs. Armstrong looked as though she were about to tumble down the stairs. Bert rushed up to help her.

"The Flyer is gone. Some of my most valuable jewelry is gone!" Mrs. Armstrong was getting hysterical.

A large crowd gathered in the entrance hall. Ross Benton ran up to Mrs. Armstrong. "My crew is at your service," he said. "We'll do anything we can to help."

"The first thing is to call the police," Bert suggested. "Ask for Lieutenant Pike, Dad," he called out as Mr. Bobbsey rushed off to the telephone.

With Ross Benton's help, Bert guided Mrs. Armstrong down the stairs and into a chair. "We've solved some mysteries ourselves," Nan said. "We'd be happy to help you."

"Thank you, dear." Mrs. Armstrong sighed. Nan could tell that she didn't really believe the Bobbseys could get back her jewels. She just didn't want to be rude.

"When did you see the Flyer last?" Nan asked.

"When I put it away, a little less than an hour ago," Mrs. Armstrong said. "I left it in my jewel case and hurried back downstairs." She shook her head.

"I guess I forgot to lock the bedroom door as I left. I was so excited about having the movie people in the house. To think, I left the door open to some thief!"

"So, the gems were stolen within the last hour," Nan said.

"We should alert the guard at the gate!" Bert said, suddenly remembering him.

"You can call him. Use the telephone near the door," Mrs. Armstrong said. "Just dial nine."

Bert phoned the guard and told him about the theft. "Has anyone left in the last hour? No?" He looked over at Mrs. Armstrong.

"And no one will!" Mrs. Armstrong walked over to the phone. "No one is to be allowed off the estate," she ordered. "Keep the gates locked until the police arrive."

Moments later, the wail of police sirens came winding up the driveway. Then Lieutenant Pike came through the door. Several police officers followed him.

"Good evening, Mrs. Armstrong," the lieutenant said. "I understand the theft was less than an hour ago. The clues should still be fresh. Let's look at the scene of the crime."

"Could we come along, sir?" Bert asked.

"Oho! The Bobbseys!" said Lieutenant Pike. "I should have expected you." He shook his head. "You know I can't let you in while we're checking out the crime scene. Suppose you just watch from the door?"

Bert and Nan followed the lieutenant and Mrs. Armstrong up the staircase. She pushed open a door to a huge room, decorated in rose-colored satins and velvets.

"I came in here about an hour ago," she said. "I put the Flyer into my jewel case, right in this small dressing room."

As the Bobbseys stood by the door, Mrs. Armstrong went to the far wall of the room.

"Don't touch anything," said Lieutenant

Pike. "We'll need to take prints from everything in the room."

"Um, Lieutenant?" Bert said. "There's something on the floor beside your foot. It looks like gold."

The lieutenant bent over and picked something up from the rug. "A small charm," he said, holding it out to Mrs. Armstrong. "Is it yours?"

"Why, no," she said.

"It's shaped like a horseshoe." Lieutenant Pike held it up to study. "And it's engraved. 'To Tim—good luck.'" He looked at Mrs. Armstrong. "Anyone named Tim at the party?"

Nan gulped. "I know one person. Tim Archer, the actor . . . but I'm sure he didn't have anything to do with the theft!"

"Tim Archer, you say?" Lieutenant Pike repeated. "Let's go down and have a talk with him."

As they reached the foot of the stairs, a police officer came up to them. "We made a list of people who were together when the crime took place," he said.

"So, these people have alibis," said Lieutenant Pike. He ran his eyes down the list.

"Keep your fingers crossed," Bert whispered to Nan. "I know whose name he's looking for."

"I don't see Tim Archer's name here." Lieutenant Pike looked around. "Where is he?"

At that moment, Tim came into the ballroom through the French doors. "Why is everyone so quiet?" he asked.

Lieutenant Pike stepped forward. "Are you Tim Archer?"

"That's right," Tim said. He looked curiously at the police officers. "What's going on?"

"I'll ask the questions," Lieutenant Pike cut in. "Do you know this charm?"

"I should," Tim said. "It looks just like mine. It's right here in my jacket. . . ." He quickly searched his blazer pockets. But they were empty.

"I guess it *is* mine," Tim said. "Maybe I dropped it out in the garden just now. Where did you find it?"

"At the scene of a crime, Mr. Archer," the lieutenant said. "The Armstrong Flyer has been stolen. And the evidence seems to point to you!"

"You've got to be kidding!" Tim said.

"We found your charm right outside the room where the jewels were kept. And where were you at the time of the crime? Out walking in the garden! Not a very good alibi." Lieutenant Pike took Tim by the arm. "I think you'd better come with me for questioning."

Murmurs spread through the crowd. "Tim Archer could have stolen the jewels!" "He's being arrested!" "He's going to jail! This is terrible!"

Ross Benton rushed up. "Lieutenant, you don't understand!" the movie man said. "We just started shooting a film with Mr. Archer. You can't take him to jail. That would mean the end of our movie!"

"We're just asking him questions—right now," said Lieutenant Pike. "We'll be questioning everyone here. Maybe someone will remember seeing him."

"*I* saw him," a small voice piped up. "He was in Mrs. Armstrong's room!"

Ross Benton whirled around. "Jessica!" he said. "How can you . . . Wait a second. You're not Jessica!"

"That's right. I'm Flossie Bobbsey, and I saw him." Flossie pointed at Tim.

"Flossie, are you sure?" Nan asked.

"Yes!" she said. "I was looking for Freddie. I knew he was hiding upstairs, so I peeked in all the rooms."

Flossie took a deep breath. "When I looked into that big, pink room, I saw Tim Archer. He was sneaking into the dressing room!"

3
Quiet on the Set!

"That's not true!" Tim protested.

"You're sure this is the person you saw?" Lieutenant Pike asked Flossie.

"Positive!" Flossie nodded her head.

"That settles it," said Lieutenant Pike. "Mr. Archer, I'm taking you in on suspicion of stealing Mrs. Armstrong's jewels. I suggest you call a lawyer."

Nan and the others stared in shock.

"But I didn't do it!" Tim said. "You can even search me! I don't have the jewels!"

"Then we'll search the house and the grounds," said Lieutenant Pike. He turned to a police officer. "Read him his rights."

"My poor movie!" Ross Benton moaned.

"My poor jewels!" Mrs. Armstrong chimed in.

"What about poor Tim?" Nan turned to Bert. "Everyone thinks he's a thief. But maybe he didn't steal the jewels. I just can't believe that he did."

Lieutenant Pike turned in the doorway. "The rest of you are free to go," he said. "But an officer at the door will search each one of you. We may have found a suspect, but I want the jewels."

He looked around again. "And, Mrs. Armstrong, I think they're still on the property. No one passed through the gates after the theft. And we haven't heard any alarms, so no one has tried to get over your fence."

Mr. and Mrs. Bobbsey appeared beside the twins. "We may as well leave," Mr. Bobbsey said. "We can't be of any further help here, and I've got an early morning tomorrow. A big shipment is coming in." Mr. Bobbsey ran a lumberyard.

Nan nodded. "That's right," she whispered to her brothers and sister. "We'll be working early, too. We have a case to solve."

The next morning found the four twins waiting in the car. Their mother hid a smile as she opened the door.

"Are you really sure you all want to come with me to Hicks Field?" she teased.

"Come on, Mom," Bert said. "You know they're filming the movie there. We want to see it."

"I don't care about the movie," Freddie said. "I want to see the balloons."

"Ha!" Flossie said. "What he really wants to do is get a ride."

Mrs. Bobbsey just shook her head. Hicks Field was right ahead now—a big, open grassy space. She parked the car at the edge.

"This is a big operation," Bert said. "Look at that equipment!"

"It won't be easy looking for clues around here," Nan whispered after counting ten big tents pitched on the open field. She got out of the car, watching the bustling movie set. Crew members pushed movie cameras around on dollies. Carpenters hammered on sets. People clustered around two balloons still tied to the ground.

One was yellow. The other was the Rainbow Clipper, the huge rainbow-colored balloon the twins had seen at Amy's party the night before. Freddie and Flossie headed straight for it.

Nan and Bert took off running. They caught up with the younger twins at the edge of a crowd.

"What's going on?" Nan asked.

"Don't know," Freddie answered, standing on his tiptoes. "Can't see."

The crowd of people shifted. The Bobbseys could see into the middle of the circle. Jessica Jordon stood in front of the balloon, talking with Ross Benton.

"She looks like she's crying," Nan said. "Let's move up."

They inched forward through the crowd. Soon they could hear what Ross Benton was saying.

"This is your last chance," he said to Jessica. "You've got to go up in that balloon."

"I'm scared," Jessica said.

"You weren't afraid to go up yesterday." Ross Benton was having a hard time holding on to his temper. "You said you *loved* it. Besides, it's in your contract. You *have* to do it."

"I changed my mind," Jessica said. "I don't like balloons. They're too dangerous."

"Dangerous?" Benton yelled. "They're *not* dangerous!"

Nan glanced at Bert. Both of them were wondering the same thing. Why was Jessica Jordon suddenly afraid of balloons?

Then Nan heard two voices in the crowd. "What if she tells them?" a woman's voice asked.

"I'll make sure she doesn't," a man's voice answered roughly.

Nan turned, trying to see who'd been talking. But there were too many people around. She listened hard, hoping to hear the voices again.

Ross Benton's yelling drowned everything out. "Oh, this is perfect," he shouted. "The police take away one star, and the other one won't work with balloons. Of course, this is a movie about balloons. But who cares?"

He threw his megaphone down and stomped on it. "What are you all looking at?" He glared at the other actors. "Do you have problems, too? Maybe I should just cancel the movie!"

Ross Benton's angry face scanned the crowd. Then he saw the Bobbseys. For a second, he stared harder. Then, looking at Flossie, he broke into a big smile.

"Come here, little girl." His voice was suddenly sweet. "I want a closer look at you."

"Who, me?" Flossie pushed behind Freddie to hide.

"Yes, you." Benton's smile grew even bigger. Flossie walked toward him.

"He's going to kick us off the set," Freddie

whispered. "Now we'll never get to ride in a balloon."

"Jessica, come here," Benton barked. "Stand beside this girl."

Jessica stepped over, standing shoulder to shoulder with Flossie. They were the same size. They had the same features. They peeked shyly at each other. They even smiled alike.

"Twins!" Benton cried. "They look like twins. What's your name?" he asked Flossie.

"Flossie. Flossie Bobbsey," she said, pronouncing her full name carefully.

"Well, Flossie Bobbsey, how would you like to be a star?"

"Me?" Flossie squealed with delight.

"You'll be Jessica's stand-in," Benton said. "The most exciting scenes in the movie will be yours—the balloon scenes." He stopped for a second. "You're not afraid of heights or anything, are you?"

"Oh, no," Flossie answered. "I'd just love to go up in one of those balloons." She turned to Freddie as if to say, "See what I got."

Jessica turned to Flossie. "I—I don't think you should go. It's not safe," she warned.

Ross Benton paid no attention. "Of course," he said, "I'll need to speak to your parents. To get their approval."

Flossie's eyes searched the crowd. She found her mother and ran toward her. "Oh, Mom, please? Please?"

"Well . . ." said Mrs. Bobbsey. "Why not?"

The crowd broke up as Benton took Mrs. Bobbsey aside. "We'll have to discuss Flossie's new career," he said with a smile.

Bert followed them. "I can't believe it!" he said.

"What do you think about it, Freddie?" Nan looked around. "Freddie?"

But Freddie was nowhere to be seen.

He was sneaking into the gondola of the big yellow balloon.

"It's not fair!" he mumbled to himself. "Flossie's going to ride in these. And they'll make a movie of it. She'll even get paid for it! No fair!"

He stared up at the big yellow cloth bag, billowing above. This is great! he thought.

A noise came from a tent near the balloon. Freddie ducked down. I thought everyone had left, he thought. What if they find me in here?

As he hid on the floor of the gondola, he heard two people walk past.

"That was a pretty piece of acting," a man's voice growled. He sounded angry.

"I wasn't acting." Freddie knew that voice. It was Jessica Jordon's! "I *am* scared."

"Well, you should be. And if you're not careful about what you say to people," the man warned, "I'll give you something you can *really* be scared about!"

4

A Scary Stunt

Freddie lay silently on the floor of the gondola. He could hardly believe his ears. Somebody was threatening Jessica Jordon! But why?

He decided to get up and risk a peek. But as he got to his feet, he heard new voices. They came from behind him. Uh-oh, he thought. He ducked down again.

"Get this one ready next," someone said. Freddie felt a kick on the side of the gondola.

Freddie gulped. He looked over the side of the basket.

"Hey, a stowaway," said a young guy with blond hair. "Out, you. No kids allowed."

"I'm sorry." Freddie climbed over the side

and jumped to the ground. "I just wanted to see what it was like. It must be really great to go ballooning."

The man grinned at Freddie's enthusiasm. "My name is Pete," he said. "And you're right. There's nothing like a hot-air flight. You don't even feel like you're moving. You just float like a cloud."

He smiled down at Freddie. "Who knows? Maybe I'll get a chance to take you up sometime."

Then his face got stern. "But no sneaking aboard. It's not safe. Especially around my boss—he'd skin you alive. So stay away from the balloons. Okay?"

"Okay," Freddie promised. "Thanks, Pete. See you later."

Freddie looked around for Jessica Jordon and the mystery man. But he was too late. Both were out of sight. He kept on looking around until he heard his name being called.

"Where have you been?" Nan asked. "You shouldn't just disappear like that."

"I didn't just disappear," Freddie said. "I saw something—"

But he'd already lost Nan. She was looking off at a police car parking on the field. In the back was Tim Archer.

Ross Benton rushed over to the car. "So, he's back?" the director said to Lieutenant Pike. "I'm glad you're finished with your . . . *questions.*"

Lieutenant Pike got out of the car. "You can have Mr. Archer back," he said. "But he can't leave town." He tapped a piece of paper in his hand. "I've also got a search warrant here. We want a look at Mr. Archer's dressing room."

Tim looked terrible. His hair was a mess, and his eyes looked tired. Nan was sure he hadn't gotten a wink of sleep in jail. "Do you think I could change into something else?" he asked. He was still in the blazer he'd worn to the party.

"After we finish looking around," said Lieutenant Pike.

One of his men came out with a piece of paper in his hand. "We found this on his makeup table, Lieutenant."

Lieutenant Pike spread out the piece of paper. "Interesting," he said. "A map."

The Bobbseys moved behind him to get a look. "It's a diagram of somebody's property," Bert said. "See the circle with an X in it in the center?"

"Look how one corner is cut off," Freddie added. "That's Kenilworth Road."

Nan's heart sank. "And that means . . ."

"That means this is a map of the Armstrong estate." Lieutenant Pike turned to Tim Archer. "Like to explain what this was doing in your dressing room?"

"I don't know!" Tim said. "It's not mine!"

"Just like that charm wasn't yours." The lieutenant shook his head. Nan could see he didn't believe Tim. "I'll tell you again, Mr. Archer. Don't leave town." He led his men away.

Shoulders sagging, Tim went into his dressing room.

"It doesn't look good for him at all," Bert whispered.

"He didn't do it. I *know* he didn't," Nan said. She looked at her brothers. "And we've got to prove it."

"That's easy enough to say." Bert shook his head. "But how do we do it?"

"Well, Flossie is working here now. So, we have a good reason to be on the set." Her face was thoughtful. "Someone worked pretty hard to frame Tim."

"Someone who could get into his dressing room," Bert added. "Maybe we should look around and see what we can find."

"Right," Freddie said. He knew just where he was going to look.

It took a little while, but he finally tracked

down Jessica Jordon. She was over by one of the sets, sitting alone in a folding chair. Freddie read her name across the back.

"I hope Flossie doesn't get one of those chairs," he said. "We'll never hear the end of it."

Jessica gave him a shy smile. "You must be Flossie's brother," she said.

"Right. I'm Freddie." He got right down to business. "I was checking out the yellow balloon before. And I heard that man scaring you."

Jessica's smile disappeared in a flash of fear. "He—he wasn't scaring me."

"Oh, yes, he was," Freddie insisted. This was just like arguing with Flossie. Jessica was even getting the same stubborn look Flossie did. Freddie sighed. This girl wasn't going to tell him anything.

"Okay, don't tell me," he said. "But you'd better be careful. That guy sounded mean." He smiled at Jessica. "And just remember, if you need help, ask us."

Jessica looked up at him. A tear rolled down her cheek. "Freddie, I'm in big trouble," she said. "I saw . . ."

All of a sudden, they were in the shade. Freddie thought that a cloud had cut off the

sunshine. But Jessica was staring up into the sky. And she looked as if she'd seen a monster.

Freddie looked up. The big yellow balloon loomed over them.

"What's the matter?" Freddie asked. "It's only—"

Something came flying out of the balloon's gondola. For a second, it seemed to drift lazily downward. Then it landed with a *whumppp!* just a few feet from them.

"They dropped a sandbag!" Freddie said. "Hey!" he yelled up at the balloon. "Watch what you're doing!"

The balloon vanished behind one of the set buildings. It was headed rapidly for the ground.

Jessica watched it disappear. She was shaking so badly, she could hardly stand up.

"Hey, come on," Freddie said. "It was just an accident."

"No," Jessica said. "He did it on purpose. I know he did."

Freddie wished he could see exactly where the balloon had landed.

They were standing on the town set. From where they stood, the set looked like a row of real buildings. But each "building" was just a front—a tall wooden wall, painted to look like stone or brick.

Freddie was beginning to get nervous. Whoever had dropped that sandbag could be hiding behind those wooden walls right now.

"Come on," he said. He grabbed Jessica's arm. "I think we'd better get out of here."

Too late! With a sound of grinding wood, one of the false fronts began to wobble. Jessica screamed as the wall came falling—fast—right at them!

5

Timber!

People came running when they heard Jessica scream. But Bert Bobbsey was the first one on the scene.

He rounded the corner, then stopped in horror. He had a perfect side view of the toppling wall. It was sure to flatten the two kids. They were running, but their legs were just too short. Bert headed for them at top speed. He dashed in, under the shadow of the falling wall. Arms spread wide, he caught Jessica and Freddie.

Two giant steps and one wild jump later, they landed in sunlight—and safety. The wall crashed down just behind them.

Ross Benton came rushing up. "Jessica! The set! What's going on?"

"I-it fell down," Freddie gasped. "Nearly squashed us."

Ross Benton stared from the fallen set to Jessica. "Are you all right?" he asked.

"I'm fine—fine," Jessica said.

"Good." The director stared at his crew. "Well? What are you all standing around here for? Get this thing back up! We have a movie to make!"

People began running in all directions. A man stopped beside Freddie. "I'm glad you weren't under there," he said.

"Pete!" Freddie said. "What happened?"

Pete shrugged. "I don't know," he said.

A gray van pulled up, and a silver-haired man leaned out. Freddie noticed that he was a really a young man—in spite of the bristly silver hair. "Hey, Pete!" he yelled. "Get a move on! We've got a balloon to catch!"

"That's the boss, Ron Keller," Pete whispered. "A real grouch!" He ran over to the van and climbed in. It roared away.

Freddie turned from the van to Jessica. Nan had arrived by now and was kneeling beside her. But Jessica still sat on the ground, staring.

"It's okay now. We're safe," Freddie said. "Can you tell us what . . ."

But just then, a young woman joined them. Nan recognized her immediately. She'd seen her the night before. She was the young woman who had cut in on Nan's dance with Tim.

"Am I glad to see you, Lara," Ross Benton said. "See if you can calm Jessica down. It would be nice to get *some* film shot today."

Lara knelt down to have a private talk with Jessica.

The little girl first looked at Lara's face. Then she threw her arms around Lara's neck and started to cry.

"Come on, Jessica. You'd better get some rest. Your eyes will be all puffy. And you have some close-ups to film today."

Lara took Jessica by the arm and led her to a tent.

Silently, the Bobbseys walked away.

They walked to their car, where they met Flossie.

"I've been looking all over for you," she said. "Where were you?"

They filled her in on what had happened. Then they all started to talk about the case.

"Okay, what have we got?" Bert asked.

"I think we have someone trying to frame Tim Archer." Nan counted points off on her fingers. "They put his lucky charm in Mrs. Armstrong's room. And a fake map in his dressing room."

"But he did it," Flossie said. "I saw him in the room."

"I've been thinking about that," Nan said. "How do you know it was Tim Archer?"

Flossie looked at her. "What do you mean? He was wearing his blazer—his pants. Who do you think it was?"

"Did you see his face?" Nan asked.

Flossie stopped for a second. "I only saw his back. But . . ."

"You didn't see his face, then."

Bert stared at Nan. "What are you saying?" he asked.

"Look around you. We're on a movie set, full of movie people. They make their livings from make-believe. From playing parts."

Bert nodded. "You think it was somebody pretending to be Tim?"

"Well, I don't think it was Tim," Nan said. "Who does that leave?"

Bert shook his head. "Too many other people."

"I know someone who could help us," Freddie said.

"Who?" Nan asked.

"Jessica Jordon," said Freddie. "I think she saw something. Maybe at the party. Whatever it was, she's really scared." He sighed. "But I don't think she'll tell me what happened."

"Maybe she'll talk to me," Flossie said. "I think she likes me."

"Okay, then," Nan said. "Flossie will stay close to Jessica and see what she can find out."

"I wonder," Bert said. "Maybe this has something to do with her being afraid of balloons." He thought for a moment. "Freddie, tell me more about the accident."

Freddie started to tell his story. "Well, it all started when the bag fell from the balloon. . . ."

"A balloon again!" Bert said. "We should check it out."

"And what about the falling wall?" Nan said. "We have a lot of things to check. Freddie, you and I should search for more clues. Bert, you should look at what happened to the wall."

"What about the jewels?" Freddie said. "Shouldn't we be trying to find them?"

"The police are searching the Armstrong estate." Nan shook her head. "We'd better work on clearing Tim. I have a feeling that will be hard enough."

"Well," Bert said, "I still think we should check out that balloon, too."

When they reached the row of fake buildings, they had a surprise. The big, yellow balloon—or what was left of it—was collapsed on the ground. The crew was flattening the gas bag, and picking up the wicker basket.

Pete the balloon man grinned at Freddie. "When I heard we had a runaway balloon, I thought I was going to find you in here," he said. "Somebody took this balloon up for a ride. I guess they thought it would be fun."

"They won't think so after I'm done with them," a voice growled.

Everyone turned around to see Ron Keller. The balloon boss ran a hand through his short, silvery hair. "I'm going to find out who was fooling around with that balloon. They not only stole it, they dropped a sandbag. When I find them, they're going to be fired."

"Hey, maybe it was just a joke, boss." Pete looked very upset. "Or an accident."

"I don't care," said Keller. "That's not the kind of accident I want on my crew."

While Keller talked, Bert walked away. He looked over one of the false fronts that was still standing. A line of wooden braces held up the painted wood.

Bert went over to the set that had fallen. His hand went into his pocket. Out came his Rex Sleuther Pocket Crime-Solver. He fiddled with

Scene
12

several of the tools. Then he swung out the magnifying glass.

Carefully, he started looking at the wooden braces. Especially where they had broken off.

"I don't like accidents," Keller said loudly. "And I don't like working on jinxed movies."

Bert suddenly spoke up. "This movie isn't jinxed," he said. "Somebody *made* that accident happen."

He pointed to the end of one of the braces. "All four of these show the same kind of break. Part of the wood is ragged."

"So?" said Keller.

"The other half of the break is straight. It was cut. Somebody sawed halfway through the wood. They they pushed against the wall until it fell."

Bert's face was puzzled. "There's no way that wall falling could be an accident. It was carefully planned. But why?"

6
Action!

"How do I look?" Flossie asked early the next morning. She sat in the front seat of the station wagon with her mother. The car had just turned onto the dirt road leading to the movie set.

"You look great," Mrs. Bobbsey answered.

"I should have worn lipstick." Flossie flipped down the car's vanity mirror and primped her hair. "Jessica wears lipstick."

Mrs. Bobbsey came up to Hicks Field, and stopped the car. "We're here," she said.

"At last!" Freddie said from the backseat.

Freddie, Bert, and Nan scrambled out of the car. Flossie stayed in the front with her mother.

"Promise you'll be back in time for my first scene?" Flossie asked. Her lower lip quivered a bit. She'd never let Freddie know, but she was feeling a little scared. Especially at the thought of going up in a balloon.

"Of course I'll be there, honey," Mrs. Bobbsey said. "Mr. Benton told me it would be at ten o'clock."

"And will you write a story about me for the paper?" Flossie took one more glance in the mirror. Freddie would really be jealous.

Mrs. Bobbsey smiled. "I'll ask my editor. He may think I'm too close to the subject." She hugged Flossie, who grinned back. "Someone else may be writing the story."

"Okay," Flossie said. "As long as you're going to be there." She hopped out of the car and blew Mrs. Bobbsey a kiss.

"Hurry up, Flossie," Freddie yelled. "Mr. Benton wants you."

Ross Benton came hurrying across the field toward her. "Our makeup artist is waiting for you," he said.

"Can I go with her?" Nan asked.

"Sure. The blue trailer near set four," Benton said. "Get there on the double."

"Yes, sir!" Flossie said. She and Nan ran for the trailer.

"We'd better knock, I guess," Nan said when they came to the door.

"Is that Flossie?" a woman's voice called out from inside. "Come on in."

"Here I am!" Flossie stepped into the trailer.

"Hi, I'm Lara." The young woman smiled and shook back her chestnut-colored hair. She was very pretty, with big, green eyes.

"Hi," said Flossie. "This is my sister Nan."

"Um, hello," Nan said. "We met at the party."

"Oh, Jessica," Flossie went on. "Hi."

Jessica Jordon was sitting in front of a makeup mirror. The light bulbs all around the sides cast a bright light on her reflection.

"I just finished making up Jessica," Lara said. "Now it's your turn. Nan, why don't you sit down and watch?"

Jessica got up, and Flossie slid into the seat. She stared at herself in the brightly lit mirror. Lara stood behind her.

"I'll give you the same face I just gave Jessica," Lara said.

"But that's her real face," Flossie said. "Isn't it?"

Lara grinned. "Not exactly. She's wearing a lot of makeup."

"Lots!" Jessica agreed. "I look really different

without Lara's help." She picked up a tiny American flag and fanned her face.

Flossie peered at her. "Oooh!" she said. "Do you have mascara on?"

"Gobs of it." Jessica batted her eyelashes and giggled. "And so will you."

She put the flag down on the table. "Don't forget to take this. You'll need it for your scene."

Flossie glanced at the flag as Lara went to work on her. Getting made up wasn't easy. Flossie had to sit still for ages. She began to wonder if being in the movie was worth it.

"Do you have any brothers or sisters?" Nan asked Jessica.

"No, I'm an only child," Jessica answered. "My mom and dad are actors, too. They're making another movie right now."

"Who takes care of you?" Flossie asked.

"Well, Lara takes care of me when she can," Jessica said. "She's my best friend."

In the mirror, Flossie saw Lara give Jessica a warm smile.

"You're lucky to be an only child," Flossie said. "You should meet my twin brother, Freddie."

"I have," Jessica said. "He—"

"Flossie! You're moving!" Lara's voice cut in.

"Will I be done soon?" Flossie asked.

"I just want to add a little more pink to your cheeks," Lara answered.

"My favorite color," Flossie said. "My bedroom is pink. So is my bicycle."

Lara put the finishing touches on Flossie's face. Then she asked Jessica to stand beside Flossie and look in the mirror.

"That's fantastic!" Nan said. "Lara, you do great work."

"I can't believe it!" Flossie burst out. "I'm Jessica Jordon!"

"And I'm Flossie Bobbsey!" Jessica said.

Both of them laughed.

"Okay, girls. You'd better hurry to the costume fitters now," Lara said. "You don't want to keep Mr. Benton waiting."

"No way," said Flossie. She headed for the door.

"You're next, Nan," Lara said. "If you'd like."

"Me?" Nan said. "You'd do a makeup job on me?"

"Sure." Lara smiled. "Would you like to look like a movie star?"

"Would I!" Nan said.

"See you later, Nan," Flossie yelled. She and Jessica ran out the door.

Twenty minutes later, Flossie and Jessica

walked out of the wardrobe tent. Both of them wore white sailor dresses.

Freddie walked by. When he saw them, he stopped and stared.

"Oh, gross. Two Flossies!" he said.

"Better than two Freddies," Flossie shot back. She smiled at Jessica. "Now I have a twin I like."

Jessica giggled.

"Flossie! Jessica!" Bert came running up. "Mr. Benton wants you on the balloon set right away."

Flossie, Jessica, and Freddie hurried after Bert. Ahead of them rose the big, rainbow-colored balloon.

"Are you afraid?" Jessica asked as they came closer.

"No way," Flossie said. "I love Ferris wheels, roller coasters, all that stuff."

"Me, too," Jessica said. She slowed down. "But I don't like balloons."

Before Flossie could ask why, Ross Benton appeared. "Okay, Flossie. In this scene, your father takes you up for a ride. He's practicing for a balloon race that has a valuable prize for the winner. As you take off, look excited and happy. Got that?"

"Excited and happy," Flossie repeated. She put on her best excited-and-happy look.

"I can't stand this," Freddie whispered to Bert.

"Fine!" Ross Benton exclaimed. "Perfect. Now, just stay here." He walked away to talk to a cameraman.

"Who plays my dad?" Flossie asked.

"Oh, he won't be here till next week," said Pete the balloon man. "I'll be taking you up." He grinned. "The cameras won't be on me. They'll be on you."

Flossie made a face at Freddie. She could see he was jealous. Then she turned back to Pete. "And who are we supposed to be racing against?"

"Me," Tim Archer said, coming up. "I'm the daring young man who tries to beat you and your dad."

"Who wins?" Bert asked.

"We're not allowed to give that away," Pete answered. "It's a secret."

"Can't you tell us?" Freddie begged.

Tim winked. "Mr. Benton hasn't told *us* yet. Some days, I think even *he* doesn't know."

"Hey, who's that?" Pete asked.

A beautiful, dark-haired girl came walking toward them. Tim whistled softly.

"Am I in time to watch?" the girl asked.

"Nan!" Bert burst out. "What happened to you?"

The gorgeous girl blushed bright red. "Lara made me over," she said. "What do you think?"

"You look great," Tim said.

"Lara turned you into a whole different person!" said Flossie.

"But Mom will have a fit," Freddie added.

Nan got even more embarrassed. "Uh-oh!" she said. "I forgot about Mom."

"Have I missed anything?" Mrs. Bobbsey came rushing up. She looked at Freddie, Flossie, and Bert. "Where's Nan?"

"Right here, Mom." Nan blushed again. Everyone on the set laughed.

Mrs. Bobbsey's jaw dropped.

"First take in five minutes!" Ross Benton bellowed. "Prepare for shooting."

"Oh, no!" Flossie whispered to Jessica. "I left that flag in Lara's trailer. I'll be right back!"

Flossie took off across the field at top speed. She ran up the steps of the trailer. Throwing open the door, she burst inside.

A man with spiky silver hair was with Lara. They were hunched over a table, talking.

The man whirled around. He stared at Flossie with hard, dark eyes.

"Bothering us again, Jessica?" he snarled. "You never learn, do you?"

7

A Yellow Clue

"We're ready now. Flossie? Flossie?" Ross Benton looked around. "Where is that girl?"

"She went back—" Freddie began.

The director cut him off. "Well, get her. Now!"

Freddie ran for the makeup trailer. The door was open.

"What are you talking about? It's *me,* Flossie." Freddie could hear that his sister's voice sounded scared.

Freddie dashed inside. He found Ron Keller glaring at his sister.

"I need the little American flag that Jessica gave me." Flossie began looking around the trailer. "I left it around here, somewhere."

The silver-haired balloon boss got out of his seat. "I'll just be in the way," he said. He pushed his chair back and stepped out the door.

"Hey, you dropped something," Freddie called after him. But Keller was already gone.

Freddie picked up a piece of bright yellow rubber from the floor. "It fell from his pocket as he was getting up," he said. He stretched the scrap of colored rubber. "I wonder what it's for."

Lara was busy helping Flossie search for the flag. "What?" she asked.

"Oh, nothing." Freddie slipped the scrap into his pocket. Maybe it was a clue. He knew he'd seen something that was yellow, just like the piece of rubber. But he couldn't figure out what it was.

"I think it was on this table. . . ." Flossie dug through a pile of black wigs. "Here it is!" she said waving the flag. Then she turned to Freddie. "Come on. I have to get back to the set."

Freddie followed as she rushed out of the trailer. Together, they jogged across the field to the set.

"I'm glad we're out of there," Freddie said.

Flossie nodded. "Boy, was that man mean," she said. "He thought I was Jessica, and he hollered at me."

They reached the balloon. Besides the movie

crew, a newspaper photographer stood in the crowd. Mrs. Bobbsey stood beside him. "Well, we're here for our story," she said.

"Great!" Flossie said. "I'll be famous!"

Mrs. Bobbsey smiled. "Enjoy your ride, sweetheart." She bent down and gave Flossie a kiss.

"Have fun, Floss," Bert called.

"It's been nice knowing you," Freddie added.

That earned him a poke from Nan's elbow. "Nothing is going to happen to Flossie," she said.

Freddie watched Flossie's face as she looked up at the balloon. She looked excited. But she also looked very, very scared.

"Hey, Flossie," Tim Archer said. "Here's a trick—just between us actors. Remember your favorite things. That way, you *can't* look bad."

He shook hands with Flossie, and she gave him a smile. The photographer took a shot of them.

"I think I'm going to be sick," Freddie whispered.

Nan grinned. "Oh, you're just jealous," she whispered back. "You wish you were the one going up."

"Clear the area, clear the area!" Ross Benton shouted through his megaphone. "Get ready for take one."

Pete, already in the gondola, lifted Flossie in beside him.

The director's assistant snapped shut a wooden board that said SCENE 40 TAKE 1. Silence fell over the set.

Flossie stood in the gondola, her eyes shining with excitement. As Pete worked the balloon's controls, a crew member released the ropes holding the balloon. It lifted off into the air.

Flossie's face broke out in a big smile. She waved her flag.

"There she goes," whispered Nan. "Up, up, and away!"

"The lucky duck," Freddie whispered back.

The *News* photographer shot picture after picture.

The rainbow-colored balloon soared into the sky.

"Cut!" Benton called to the cameraman. "Got it in the first take! Next, we do Tim's launch scene. Come on, people!"

The crew hurried off. But Nan kept her eyes on the balloon carrying Flossie.

"It looks only as big as a baseball now," Bert said. Soon, the balloon would disappear over the horizon.

"Wait a minute!" Freddie said. "How will Flossie get back?"

"The balloon crew follows in a van," Bert said. "Your friend Pete explained it to me. They can predict the landing spot by knowing the direction of the wind. Flossie should be back here in about two hours."

"We have to get back to the *News,*" Mrs. Bobbsey said. "Nan, will you meet Flossie when she comes back? Tell her how proud I was to watch her."

"Sure, Mom," Nan said. "Just remember what Flossie would like." She grinned. "A front-page photo in tonight's *Lakeport News.*"

Mrs. Bobbsey laughed.

"Well, I've got some great shots here." The photographer tapped his camera and grinned, too.

The kids waved goodbye.

"What do we do now?" Bert asked.

"Let's go where the action is," Nan said.

They all strolled over to the setup for the next scene. "Looks like Tim is going to take off now," Bert said.

Tim Archer stood in the gondola of the yellow balloon, making a speech. As the Bobbseys got closer to the set, they passed a large movie camera on a dolly. One of the crew members was tinkering with it.

The workman stepped back, smiling and

wiping his hands. His eyes were on the camera, not on where he was going. Before Bert realized what was happening, the man bumped into him.

"Oops! Sorry," said the man. "A little doohickey in there got jammed. I finally loosened it up."

"Wow," Freddie said. "That looks like some camera."

"Sure is," the man said. "Want a look through it?"

He helped Freddie up to the eyepiece. "It's even pointed in the right direction for this scene. Take a peek."

Just as Freddie looked through the camera, Tim's balloon launched. The camera lens somehow made the yellow balloon seem smaller as it rose up. It almost looked like a toy.

Freddie suddenly jerked back from the eyepiece. "What's the matter?" the man asked.

"Oh, nothing," Freddie said quickly. "I was just thinking." He looked over at the set. The film crew was breaking up again, moving on to another scene.

"Where's Jessica?" Freddie suddenly asked. "I've got to talk to her—right now!"

8
Up, Up, and Away

Flossie peered over the side of the gondola. The fields around Lakeport spread out below her. They looked like a patchwork quilt of greens and browns.

"Flossie, please do me a favor," Pete said. "Don't lean so far out. You're not wearing a parachute, you know."

Quickly, Flossie sat down in the bottom of the gondola. As she did, a shiny glint caught her eye. Something was wedged in the wicker floor of the gondola. She knelt down to examine it.

"Ooooh, look!" she cried. "There's a gold ring down here."

"What?" Pete said. All his attention was on the balloon's controls. "It's probably a piece of costume jewelry from another movie."

Flossie worked at prying the ring loose. "It doesn't want to come . . . out!" she grunted. Finally, the ring popped free. Flossie held it up to the sunlight.

"Wow, it sure is beautiful," she said.

Pete glanced over. "That looks like a ruby."

Flossie started to try the ring on. Then she stopped.

"Hey, there are letters inside. L.E.A."

"I wonder what they can stand for." Pete left the controls to look at the ring.

Flossie's eyes got big. "How about Lilian Armstrong?"

Pete stared at the ring. "You may be right," he said. "As soon as we get on the ground, you should call Mrs. Armstrong. Find out if she had a ring like this."

"But how did the ring get here?" Flossie asked. "Maybe it fell from somebody's pocket." She sat for a moment, trying to think like a detective. "Who else has been in this balloon?"

"We can't find out until we get back to the set." Pete looked at his watch. "We're supposed to meet the pickup van in twenty minutes. But the wind is stronger than I expected. I'm going to start bringing us down right now."

"How do you do that?" Flossie asked.

"Hot air is what keeps this balloon up," Pete explained. "Hot air is lighter than the air outside. And the flame from this gas burner is what makes the air hot." He turned the flame off.

"Now, we could just let the air cool naturally. But to get down faster, I can pull this cord. It opens a vent in the balloon."

He pulled on the cord, and the balloon made a sudden drop.

"Boy," Flossie said. "That really works!"

"We'll be on the ground in about ten minutes," Pete said.

Flossie sighed. "I'm sorry it's over."

The pickup van drove up to find them waiting in an empty field. The front door flew open, and Ron Keller jumped out. Another member of the balloon crew got out on the other side.

"Let's get this thing wrapped up and into the van." Keller looked at his watch. "Mr. Benton is in a hurry today."

They deflated the balloon and folded it up.

"Look what I found in the balloon!" Flossie held up the ring in front of Ron Keller as Pete and the other crew member carried the balloon and the gondola to the van. Keller stopped dead.

"What's that?" he asked.

"I think it's one of Mrs. Armstrong's jewels. Hey!" Flossie yelled as Ron Keller snatched it from her hand.

"We'd better get this to the cops. Right away." Ron Keller hurriedly got into the driver's seat. "Come on!"

They piled aboard, and Ron Keller hit the gas. The van lunged forward.

"Hey, Keller, what's the big idea?" Pete asked.

But Keller didn't answer. And he didn't slow down. He zoomed back to the movie set at breakneck sped. Half an hour later, the van screeched to a stop. Flossie jumped out, glad she was still alive.

Keller ran off at top speed. Boy, is he in a hurry to call the police, she thought. Then she began looking around the set for Bert, Nan, and Freddie.

"Just my luck," Freddie grumbled. "Jessica's filming all afternoon."

"Well, she's the only star they have left on the set," Nan said. "Tim is off flying in a balloon—

and so is Flossie." She grinned at Freddie, rubbing it in. "What did you want to ask her?"

He smiled mysteriously. "You'll find out."

Jessica's scene finally ended. Freddie rushed forward, but he was still too late. "Fix Jessica's makeup," Ross Benton ordered. "And hurry! I want to keep shooting in this light."

Jessica ran off to the makeup trailer before Freddie could talk to her.

"Rats!" said Freddie.

He was still waiting for Jessica to return when Flossie raced up.

"You'll never guess!" Flossie said.

"What?" Bert asked. Freddie was hardly listening.

"I found a clue in the balloon!" Flossie exclaimed. "It's a . . ."

"Where did Jessica go now?" Ross Benton's voice thundered. "This light isn't going to last much longer."

He came marching down from the makeup trailer. "I thought she went for makeup," he said. "But nobody's there. What am I going to do?"

Benton stopped short when he saw Flossie. "Of course!" he shouted. "I'll use you for this scene, Flossie. Report to the crew on the far side of the field—now."

"But—" Flossie began.

"No buts!" Benton shouted. "This is a very simple scene. All you have to do is run across that field into the arms of your father. Pretend he's me. I'll be standing right in front of the cameraman. Now head over to the far side of the field—on the double!"

Flossie shrugged and started running.

"I wonder what she was going to tell us," Nan said.

"Well, we'll find out in a few minutes," Bert said. "It can't have been too important. I mean, they were up in a balloon. What kind of clue could you find there?"

"Oh, you may be surprised," said Freddie.

"That's sure a long run," Nan said. Flossie had finally reached the film crew at the far end of the field. Then the director waved his arms to signal the cameraman to start shooting.

Flossie began to run back to the cameras, where Ross Benton waited for her.

Suddenly, Bert grabbed Nan's hand in alarm. "What's that balloon doing?"

The Bobbseys turned to watch the Rainbow Clipper. Moments ago, it had been roped to the ground. Now it was moving.

"Hey, it's heading toward Flossie!" Nan exclaimed. "Mr. Benton didn't say anything about that."

The huge balloon glided along the ground. A

stiff breeze was blowing it straight into Flossie's path.

"Something's wrong!" Bert started running forward.

But the balloon was already in front of Flossie. She stopped in surprise.

Then a man popped up in the gondola.

"Who's that?" cried Freddie.

"It—it looks like Tim!" Nan gasped. "I can't see his face. But that hair . . ."

The man's long arms shot out and grabbed Flossie!

Everyone was too far away. They all watched helplessly as Flossie was pulled into the gondola.

"Help!" she yelled. "Let go of me!" Her little arms flailed as she struck at the man. They leaned dangerously out of the gondola.

Then the man's hair came away in her hand!

The black wig fluttered down as the balloon shot up. The mystery man had spiky silver hair!

"Ron Keller!" gasped Nan. "What's he doing?"

"He's getting away—and we can't stop him!" Bert said grimly.

Above them, the balloon rapidly disappeared.

9

A Crash Course in Flying

"Did you see?" Bert turned to the others. "There were two other people in the gondola. One of them was Jessica!"

"Cut! Cut!" Ross Benton screamed. "What's going on here?"

"Keller's got Flossie—and Jessica!" Bert said.

"But why?" Benton asked.

"The robbery—it has to be the robbery!" Nan said. "Flossie said she found a clue in the balloon."

"Call the police! Get Pete over here!" Benton commanded.

"Let's get that wig, too," Nan said.

Pete told them about Flossie finding the ruby ring in the gondola.

"But how could any of Mrs. Armstrong's jewelry get into the balloon?" Benton burst out. "The Rainbow Clipper was fifty feet off the ground the night of the party! We would have noticed if it landed."

"The balloon didn't come down," Freddie said. "The jewels went up."

"*What?*" Everyone turned to him.

"It happened while I was going up to Chip Armstrong's room. I looked out the window and saw one of those party-favor balloons floating by. A yellow one."

Freddie shrugged. "I just thought some kid lost his balloon. But now I think I was seeing Mrs. Armstrong's jewels—flying up to the big balloon."

"That's a pretty serious thing to say," said Benton. "Especially without proof."

Freddie reached into his pocket. "What does this look like?" he asked.

Everyone looked at the piece of yellow rubber in his hand.

"It doesn't look like anything to me," Benton said.

"How about a piece of balloon?" Freddie asked. "It fell out of Ron Keller's pocket."

"Ron Keller!" said Nan. "He was up in the balloon that night. And he's the one who grabbed Flossie. When the wig came off, we all saw that silver hair."

"But why the wig?" Benton wanted to know.

"A disguise," Nan said. She thought for a second. "Maybe he thought Flossie was the only one knew about the ring. If she told everyone about it, people would start connecting the stolen jewels with the balloon—and him. So, he hid his silver hair. Then he got the clue—and Flossie—and took off."

She held the wig up. "Did you notice something else about this? It looks just like Tim Archer's hair. I think it was used before—to frame Tim for the robbery."

"Right," Bert said. "Suppose the person who stole the jewels wore this wig and a blazer. He'd look just like Tim Archer."

"But who would do that?" asked Benton.

"Think about it," Nan said. "Somebody used to making up other people's faces. Somebody with lots of wigs around . . ."

"Lara!" Bert said. "She was dancing close to Tim at the party. I'll bet she could have gotten his lucky charm."

Nan nodded. "I remember when I saw them dancing together. I noticed they were exactly the same height."

"And I saw her with Keller," said Freddie. "He was in the makeup trailer when he lost the piece of balloon."

Ross Benton shook his head. "It sounds crazy, but it all seems to hold together. Except for one thing. Why did they take Jessica?"

"I think she saw something at the party," Freddie said. He told about the threatening conversation he'd overheard. "But I didn't see who was scaring her."

"It must have been Ron Keller!" said Nan. "And that's why she wouldn't go up in the balloons. He ran the balloon crew, and she was afraid of him."

With a whine of sirens, three police cars arrived. Lieutenant Pike strode up. "Did I get this right?" he said. "Flossie's been kidnapped in a balloon?"

"Flossie *and* Jessica Jordon," Bert said. "The question is, how can we catch up with them?"

Pete spoke up. "I've figured out the wind speed and the direction. I can guide you."

"Then let's go," said the lieutenant. "If you kids want to come along, get into the car."

The Bobbseys piled into the police car, which then shot off cross-country.

"Poor Flossie," Freddie whispered. "I wonder where she is right now."

★　★　★

At that moment, Flossie was sitting in the balloon gondola. She and Jessica were huddled together. "I went out in the garden during the party," Jessica said. "And I saw Tim sending a balloon up. Then he turned around, and it wasn't Tim. It was Lara."

"Did you ask what she was doing there?" Flossie asked.

"She said she was dressed up for a joke." Jessica shook her head. "And that she was just sending a sandwich up to Mr. Keller."

"But it wasn't!" Flossie said. "She was sending the jewels up in the little balloon!"

"I know. But Lara was my friend. I couldn't tell on her." She looked absolutely miserable.

Lara knelt beside the girls. "I'm sorry you had to be so scared," she told Jessica. "When Ron and I came to Hollywood we were going to be stars. Instead, we wound up working behind the camera. Well, those jewels were going to make us rich. Rich enough to make our own movies. That's why I stole them."

Flossie stared at her. "But how come I saw Tim Archer?" She thought for a second. "Oh . . ."

Lara sighed. "You saw *me,* made up to look like Tim."

Flossie nodded. She knew Lara could make

her look like Jessica. So why couldn't she make herself look like Tim Archer?

"It was all *my* idea," Ron Keller broke in. "A good thief always sets a trap for someone else. I had Lara steal Tim's good-luck charm. With that planted in the bedroom and her looking like him, he was sure to get blamed."

He ran a hand through his spiky hair. "It was a perfect plan. And two dumb kids have to come along and ruin it."

"You made just one mistake," Flossie said. "You dropped the ruby ring."

"That's not the only mistake." Lara looked at Ron Keller with angry eyes. "I made a bigger one. I got mixed up in this crazy deal in the first place. Now I'm sorry I did." She hugged Jessica, who was crying softly.

"Well, it's too late now," Keller said. Flossie watched him turn up the gas burner. The balloon shot up as the air heated.

"We're making great time," he said, staring down at the ground below. "We'll be in another state before they start looking for us."

"What are you going to do with me?" Flossie said bravely. "And Jessica?"

"I haven't figured that out yet." Keller scowled at her. "I just had to get the two of you off the set before you blabbed."

"Pete knows all about the ruby ring," Flossie said. "I'll bet he's told everybody. And my brother Bert is figuring out how to save me right now!"

Keller gave a nasty laugh. "You can forget about that. We've got a good, stiff wind. Nobody could follow us on the ground."

Flossie looked out the gondola. She could see how fast they were moving. Lakeport was already far away. Below them was a checkerboard of open fields. Gray ribbons—roads—ran through the farmland. Sometimes she saw a patch of woods.

All of it went by very quickly. Flossie realized her chances of rescue were getting smaller by the minute.

Keller moved away from the burner. He stretched and sat down in the bottom of the gondola.

Flossie glanced over at the balloon's controls. Pete had shown her how they worked. She remembered how he had pulled on the vent cord. And how they had lost altitude so quickly. She began to form a plan. *If I can wait for the right moment.*

"Lara, come over here," Keller ordered. "We have to talk." He glanced at Jessica. "Stay over there with your friend."

"This is all my fault," Jessica whispered. "If it weren't for me, you wouldn't be here."

"Don't worry," whispered Flossie. "I know how to get us down."

"How?" Jessica asked nervously.

Flossier lowered her voice still further. "I'm going to turn off the burner and pull the vent cord. Then we'll go down—fast. But I can't do it if they're watching me. Can you do something to get their attention?"

"Sure I can," Jessica said. "I'm an actress, remember?"

"Okay. Go for it," Flossie said.

Jessica got to her feet. She clutched at her stomach and groaned. Then she stumbled over to the other side of the gondola. "I'm getting sick!" she cried.

Keller and Lara stared at her in alarm. They didn't notice Flossie slipping over to the controls.

She switched off the burner. Then, grabbing the vent cord, she gave it a hard jerk. The balloon immediately began to drop.

Flossie grabbed the side of the gondola. They were falling faster than she'd expected. Maybe she'd pulled that cord too hard! She turned to Jessica, her eyes wide with fear.

"Hurry, Ron," Lara screamed as the earth

came zooming up. "You've got to slow us down!"

Keller frantically went to work on the controls.

Flossie gulped as she stared down. What had she done? They were close to the ground now—*too* close. They were going to crash!

10
Touchdown

"Get down, girls," Lara yelled. "We're going to hit!"

Flossie and Jessica held each other tightly. Then they saw the tops of trees. Seconds later, the gondola hit the earth with a thud.

For a moment, everyone stared at each other in shocked silence.

Then a relieved smile spread across Flossie's face. "Hey!" she said. "We made it!"

Flossie and Jessica scrambled out of the gondola. Flossie's first idea was to run—fast. Then she saw how shaken Jessica looked and knew they wouldn't get very far.

Lara followed the girls onto firm ground while Ron Keller fiddled with the controls. He shook his head. "No time to fill this up again," he said. He leaped out of the gondola. "We've got to get out of here."

He reached over and grabbed Flossie's arm. "You think you're smart, huh? Well, I'm not finished with you. Not yet. You and Jessica will be our hostages. And we'll get away clean."

"No!" Lara's voice was tight as she pushed Keller's hand away. "You're not taking them with you!" She stepped in front of the girls.

"Come on, Lara, knock it off." Keller scowled. "You're in this with me, so you'd better do what I say. We'll be safer if we bring them along."

"If you take those kids, I'll turn you in—first chance I get." Lara's voice was steady now. "I mean it, Ron. I've made enough mistakes with you. But I'm not going to make this one!"

Ron Keller stepped back.

"Oh, Lara," Jessica said with a sob. "We'll always stay friends, won't we? No matter what?"

Lara gave the girl a smile. "Friends forever," she said.

Ron Keller had gone back into the gondola. Flossie watched him open a small box set in the floor. He lifted a small heavy sandbag out of the box. "C'mon, Lara," he called. "Let's get out of here."

The wail of a police siren suddenly cut through the air. Keller dropped the sandbag as he clambered out of the gondola.

Seconds later, the police cars appeared on the country lane at the end of the clearing the balloon had landed in. They were heading straight for the balloon.

"Bert did it!" Flossie said. "I knew he would save us!"

"Run!" Keller shouted in panic. He bent to grab the sandbag. But as the police cars came closer, he dropped the bag and took off.

"Head for the woods!" He took Lara's arm and pulled her into the cover of the trees.

"Oh, Flossie." Jessica's voice trembled. "I hope she'll be okay."

The police cars came to a stop at the edge of the woods. The officers jumped out and went in pursuit of Keller and Lara. Bert, Nan, and Freddie spilled out, too. They ran to hug Flossie. Pete got out last and went to check the balloon.

"Are you okay?" Freddie asked anxiously.

"Of course I am," Flossie answered. "What do you think?"

Jessica told the whole story of how Flossie had foiled the kidnapping.

Just as she got to the part where the balloon had crashed, the police came back out of the woods. With them were Ron Keller and Lara—in handcuffs.

"Poor Lara," Jessica said, fighting back tears.

"Don't worry," Flossie comforted her. "I bet she'll help the police. And then they'll help her."

"You're a good friend, Flossie," said Jessica.

"And a brave little kid," Bert said.

"Well, we cleared Tim," Nan said. "Too bad we couldn't find the jewels."

"Oh, *that*," Flossie said. She bent down and grabbed the sandbag. Dragging it over to Bert, she said, "Can you get this open?"

Bert grunted as he picked up the bag. "Oof! Come on, Flossie. This is just sand and stuff."

"Open it," Flossie insisted.

Bert shrugged and pulled out his Rex Sleuther Pocket Crime-Solver. He chose the saw-toothed blade and cut into the bag.

Sand came spilling out. Then came something shiny.

"That's the Armstrong Flyer!" Nan exclaimed.

More pieces of jewelry tumbled out with the sand. Soon a pile of sparkling jewels glittered on the ground. Lieutenant Pike and several police officers gathered around.

"I don't believe this," Bert said. He shook his head. "How did you know?"

"After we crashed, Ron Keller grabbed that bag. And even though it was heavy, he tried to run with it." Flossie smiled. "I figured it must be really important."

"And it was such a perfect hiding place!" Nan said.

Pete came back from looking at the balloon. He slapped Freddie on the back. "So, you kids solved the whole mystery," he said. "Congratulations!" Freddie grinned. "And I think you deserve a reward. I'm sure Mr. Benton won't mind if I take you all for a nice balloon ride."

Freddie's grin got bigger. "All *right!*" he said.

Flossie picked up a big emerald ring from the pile of jewelry. She slipped it on her finger. Then she held her hand out to admire it.

"You know, I've been thinking," she said. "Maybe I should give up my acting career."

Nan, Freddie, and Bert stared.

"Well, after all, Ron Keller is gone. Jessica won't be afraid of balloons anymore." Flossie took off the ring and put it back.

"And, anyway . . ." Her eyes twinkled. "My family needs me. How could they go on—without their best detective!"

227

_____**PUNKY BREWSTER AT CAMP CHIPMUNK**
        Ann Matthews 62729/$2.50

_____**THE DASTARDLY MURDER OF DIRTY PETE**
        Eth Clifford 55835/$2.50

_____**ME, MY GOAT, AND MY SISTER'S WEDDING**
        Stella Pevsner 66206/$2.75

_____**JUDGE BENJAMIN: THE SUPERDOG RESCUE**
        Judith Whitelock McInerney 54202/$2.50

_____**DANGER ON PANTHER PEAK**
        Bill Marshall 61282/$2.50

_____**BOWSER THE BEAUTIFUL**
        Judith Hollands   63906/$2.50

_____**THE MONSTER'S RING**
        Bruce Colville   64441/$2.50

_____**KEVIN CORBETT EATS FLIES**
        Patricia Hermes   63790/$2.50

_____**ROSY COLE'S GREAT AMERICAN GUILT CLUB**
        Sheila Greenwald   63794/$2.50

_____**ME AND THE TERRIBLE TWO**
        Ellen Conford   63666/$2.50

_____**THE CASE OF THE HORRIBLE SWAMP MONSTER**
        Drew Stevenson   62693/$2.50

_____**WHO NEEDS A BRATTY BROTHER?**
        Linda Gondosh   62777/$2.50

_____**FERRET IN THE BEDROOM, LIZARDS IN THE FRIDGE**
        Bill Wallace   63264/$2.50

200 Old Tappan Rd., Old Tappan, N.J. 07675

Please send me the books I have checked above. I am enclosing $_____ (please add 75¢ to cover postage and handling for each order. N.Y.S. and N.Y.C. residents please add appro-priate sales tax). Send check or money order--no cash or C.O.D.'s please. Allow up to six weeks for delivery. For purchases over $10.00 you may use VISA: card number, expiration date and customer signature must be included.

Name _____

Address _____

City _____ State/Zip _____

VISA Card No. _____ Exp. Date _____

Signature _____ 724